Dear mouse friends,
Welcome to the world of

Geronimo Stilton

THE RODENT'S GAZETTE
EDITORIAL STAFF

Geronimo Stilton
A learned and brainy
mouse; editor of
The Rodent's Gazette

Thea Stilton
Geronimo's sister and
special correspondent at
The Rodent's Gazette

Trap Stilton
An awful joker;
Geronimo's cousin and
owner of the store
Cheap Junk for Less

Benjamin Stilton
A sweet and loving
nine-year-old mouse;
Geronimo's favorite
nephew

Geronimo Stilton

THE HAWAIIAN HEIST

Scholastic Inc.

The publisher does not have any control over and does not assume any responsibility for author or third-party websites or their content.

GERONIMO STILTON names, characters, and related indicia are copyright, trademark, and exclusive license of Atlantyca S.p.A. All rights reserved. The moral right of the author has been asserted. Based on an original idea by Elisabetta Dami. geronimostilton.com

Published by Scholastic Inc., *Publishers since 1920*, 557 Broadway, New York, NY 10012. SCHOLASTIC and associated logos are trademarks and/or registered trademarks of Scholastic Inc.

Stilton is the name of a famous English cheese. It is a registered trademark of the Stilton Cheese Makers' Association. For more information, go to www.stiltoncheese.com.

No part of this publication may be reproduced, stored in a retrieval system, or transmitted in any form or by any means, electronic, mechanical, photocopying, recording, or otherwise, without written permission of the copyright holder. For information regarding permission, please contact: Atlantyca S.p.A., Via Leopardi 8, 20123 Milan, Italy; e-mail foreignrights@atlantyca.it, atlantyca.com.

ISBN 978-1-338-30623-1

Text by Geronimo Stilton
Original title *Ahi, ahi, ahi, che avventura alle Hawaii!*
Cover by Iacopo Bruno, Andrea Da Rold, and Alessandro Muscillo
Illustrations by Danilo Loizedda, Antonio Campo, and Daria Cerchi
Graphics by Michela Battaglin

Special thanks to Anna Bloom
Translated by Anna Pizzelli
Interior design by Kay Petronio

10 9 8 7 6 5 4 3   19 20 21 22 23

Printed in U.S.A.   40
First printing 2019

YOU NEED A VACATION!

In August, the air on Mouse Island is as hot and sticky as a melting cheese stick. Sweat dripped off my whiskers and splat onto the asphalt under my bicycle wheels.

"I'm FRYING like a feta fritter under this sun!" I cried, panting as I pedaled slowly up a hill.

All around me, New Mouse City rodents were beating the heat any way they could: some mice walked close to the walls to get some shade, others waved fans, and some POURED cold water from street fountains right over their ears!

To keep myself **cool**, I was wearing a special helmet with a built-in umbrella. I had also installed a fan on my handlebars, which was powered by my pedaling. It was **HARD WORK**!

But it was nothing compared to the work I'd have to do when I got home. Oh, I forgot to introduce myself! My name is Stilton, *Geronimo Stilton*, and I am the editor in chief of *The Rodent's Gazette*, the most famouse newspaper on Mouse Island.

Pant! Pant!

Most of *The Rodent's Gazette* employees had already left for their summer vacations, but not me. When you're the big cheese, like I am, you have to keep your whiskers to the grindstone!

As I rounded the corner to my house, a huge billboard came into view. It showed a marvemouse-looking beach with white sand, bright blue sky, and crystal clear **water**. A surfer mouse perched on a perfect **WAVE**.

It said:

YOU NEED A VACATION!
COME TO HAWAII!

Crusty cheddar muffins, did I ever!

"I have work to do!" I huffed to the billboard. The news waits for no mouse! I SCREECHED to a halt outside my house.

Hmmph!
YOU NEED A VACATION!
COME TO HAWAII!
DO YOU RECOGNIZE THIS MOUSE?

I locked up my bicycle and struggled through the door with all my *books* and papers.

Inside, my office was barely cooler than the **outside** had been. You could have fried a slice of provolone on my computer!

It's so hot!

I set up a *fan* in the window and pointed it right at my desk. I tied an *ice* pack to my head like a hat and set out a bucket of *ice* to rest my sweaty paws in. Then I prepared a refreshing **tropical** juice drink with a colorful little umbrella. Even if I didn't have time for an actual Hawaiian vacation, I could *pretend* like I was on a Hawaiian vacation!

Suddenly, the fan sputtered and died. Grumbling, I marched over to the window to fix it. I banged on it with my paw and it started working again. But then I realized the roar was actually coming from outside!

A bright yellow **AIRPLANE** zoomed very low past my window. The plane pulled an ocean-blue banner behind it that read:

"Moldy mozzarella, there's no time for that!" I said, sitting back down at my desk. "My paws are tied! I have to get this issue out!"

I worked for a long time, until the boiling sun finally sank behind the clouds like a pat of butter on a pile of cheesy pasta.

"Mmm, that reminds me — I'm hungry! Time for a break!" I rose and **STRETCHED** my paws above my head.

I sat in front of the **TV** to watch the news and eat some **CHEESE AND CRACKERS**. When I turned on the TV, a program I'd never seen before was starting.

A mouselet wearing a **YELLOW** flowered shirt stood on a white sand beach.

Do you recognize this mouse?

"You need a vacation! Come to Hawaii!" she called.

Holey Swiss cheese! Hawaii again?!

YOU NEED A VACATION! COME TO HAWAII!

The mouselet continued. "Working too hard? Finding it **DIFFICULT** to relax? Come to Hawaii on vacation!"

I turned the TV off. "No, no, no! I have work to do!" But just as I was headed back to my desk, the doorbell rang. "Now what?" I muttered. I marched over to the front door and yanked it open. "What do you want —" I stopped.

It wasn't a mouse on my doorstep — it was a **GIGANTIC** palm tree! Hanging from the palm tree's leaves were a lot of small packages, each one of them wrapped in bright YELLOW paper.

"Jumping Jack cheese!" I cried. "What in New Mouse City is the meaning of this?"

I eagerly **OPENED** all the packages. They contained:

1. A BATHING SUIT

A STRAW HAT 2.

3. A BOTTLE OF SUNSCREEN

A PAIR OF FLIP-FLOPS 4.

5. A HAWAII TOUR GUIDEBOOK

AN AIR BANANAS PLANE TICKET TO HAWAII . . . WITH MY NAME ON IT! 6.

I looked up and spotted a **CARD** hanging from the palm tree. It read:

YOU NEED A VACATION! COME TO HAWAII!

I snorted in frustration. What kind of cat-and-mouse game was someone playing? "I have work to do!" I shouted.

Suddenly, I heard the sound of something

HERCULE POIRAT

Hercule is my childhood friend. He's a private detective and runs a very well-known detective agency in New Mouse City.

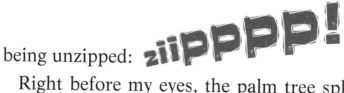

being unzipped: **ziiPPPP!**

Right before my eyes, the palm tree split in half and **HERCULE POIRAT** appeared!

"Geronimo Stilton! My old **cheese** friend! How can I convince you that you could really use a vacation in Hawaii?"

YES OR NO?

I shook my head so hard my whiskers nearly fell off. "I don't have time for games, Hercule." I turned to go back inside.

"Don't be like that, Geronimo!" Hercule exclaimed. "Think about it for a minute before you say **YES** or **NO**."

"I can't go on **VACATION** right now. I have too much to do! There are deadlines —"

But Hercule cut me off. "Enough about deadlines. You're as pale and wobbly as a blob of fresh **MOZZARELLA**. You need rest and sunshine. I've worked my tail off to convince you — please say yes!"

"What do you mean?" I asked.

DIDN'T YOU RECOGNIZE ME?

FIRST, I HID ON THE BILLBOARD...

THEN I FLEW PAST YOUR WINDOW...

THEN I PRETENDED TO BE A
TV NEWS ANCHORMOUSE...

AND FINALLY I SEALED MYSELF IN
THIS PALM TREE TO DELIVER TICKETS
FOR YOUR HAWAIIAN VACATION!

I crossed my paws in front of me. "My answer is **NO**!"

"But it's my birthday!" **HERCULE** cried. "I need a **friend** to help me celebrate in style." He grinned.

"Your birthday already passed," I said. I turned and stomped back into my house.

But Hercule would not give up. "Let's **CeLeBRate**  your birthday, instead! We'll eat cheese sandwiches by the pool, swim with dolphins, learn to surf — it will be the best **BIRTHDAY** you've ever had!"

This was getting ridiculous. "I already had my birthday, too! You even came to my party! And I don't want to do any of those things. I want to finish my work!"

Hercule's whiskers drooped. He dropped to his knees and clasped his paws together. "Okay, I lied about my BIRTHDAY. I'll tell you the truth — I need your help!"

Now I had no CHOICE! my friend needed me!

"The biggest case ever has fallen right in my lap, and I can't solve it ALONE. Will you come to Hawaii and help me? Please?"

I sighed. I couldn't say no to that! So I nodded. "Okay . . . I will help you!"

A FRIEND
OF A FRIEND

Hercule leaped up off his knees, elated. He grabbed my **paws** and spun me around until my brains felt like cottage cheese. "**THANK YOU!**"

"You're welcome, Hercule!" I cried, staggering across the room to grab hold of my desk. "Now tell me more about this case. What's so **important** that you need my help?"

"Well, my cousin Brutella Hercule's **FRIEND** vacationed in **HAWAII** last year. And this friend became friends with a *jewelry* designer there. Brutella met her at a party when she came to New Mouse City on business, and they became friends. And now she needs **HELP**!"

HAWAII

Hawaii is an archipelago in the Pacific Ocean. There are eight main islands: Niihau, Kauai, Oahu, Molokai, Lanai, Maui, Kahoolawe, and the Island of Hawaii. Hawaii is the largest island and is known as the "Big Island" to distinguish it from the entire state. Hilo is the biggest city on the Big Island.

My head was spinning. "Wait, who?"

Hercule frowned. "If you're going to help with the investigation, you have to keep up! Don't just sit there like a blob of MELTED Gouda!"

Before I could sputter a reply, Hercule continued. "The who doesn't matter — it's all about the what! This jewelry designer friend of Brutella is marvemousely talented. Her name is Kealoha, and she's becoming famouse for her nature-inspired creations. She has designed a special piece of *jewelry* inspired by a Hawaiian flower garland called the lei for the wedding of a celebrity couple."

LEI

A LEI IS A GARLAND MADE OF FLOWERS.

"That's very interesting, but what does it have to do with you?" I asked impatiently.

"I'm getting to that!" Hercule snapped. "I'm going to Hawaii because some rascally rodent has tried to STEAL it three times."

① The first time the thief tried coming in through the window . . .

② Then the thief tried to get in through the backyard . . .

③ Finally, the thief tried to disable the alarm . . .

Moldy mozzarella! *This must be some necklace,* I thought to myself.

"Obviously, the thief is determined. I promised Brutella and **KEALOHA** that I'd help keep the necklace safe and track down the would-be thief. That's why I need you, Geronimo Stilton! Trustworthy, loyal, **smart** — and the only mouse I know that's not already on vacation!"

Hercule chuckled as my fur flushed **RED** in annoyance, but he stopped suddenly and looked at his watch. "Slimy Swiss cheese! We have to move fast — our flight is leaving soon!"

I clutched my paws together. "How long do I have to pack?"

Hercule looked at his **WATCH** again. "Exactly . . . seventeen minutes and forty-two seconds."

"**WHAT?!**" I squeaked.

Hercule tossed me an empty bag from the

corner of the room. "No time for talking! Stop **mouseing** around and let's get going!" He started his timer, and I took off running.

I ran around the house like my fur was on

FIRE trying to pack my bag.

"One minute left!" Hercule called.

"*SQUEAK!*"

I had just finished tossing the essentials in my bag (extra vest, sunblock, cheese sticks), **when** Hercule's timer sounded.

"**HAWAII**, here we come!" he cried, propelling me out the door.

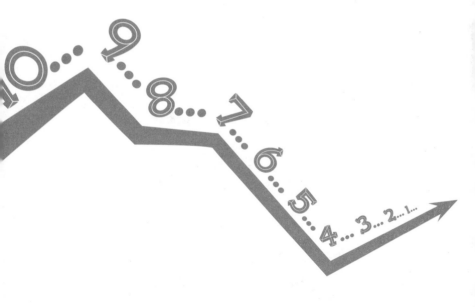

AirMouse

We made it to the airport just in time. I was so tired that I plopped myself down, belly down, on my **SUITCASE** to catch my breath.

Hercule pulled me by my tail: "Wake up, cheesebrain! This is no time for a **NAP**! Our **PLane** is about to take off!"

Just then, an announcement screeched from the loudspeaker: "*Flight number 3478 to Hilo boarding now at* **GATE** *four!*"

"Holey cheese, that's our flight!" Hercule squeaked. "**Hurry Up** or we will miss it!"

I was too tired to move, so **HERCULE** piled the suitcases on the luggage cart with me and rushed us to the **GATE**.

I could hear all the rodents in the terminal WHISPERING and laughing.

"That mouse on the luggage cart . . . isn't that Geronimo Stilton, the *famouse* writer? Why is he being wheeled around like a **block of cheese**?"

We BOARDED the plane just in time! As soon as we buckled our seat belts, the pilot made an announcement: "We are expecting **turbulence** during the flight,

so please keep your seat belts **FASTENED** at all times. We're in for a bumpy ride. I hope nobody on board gets airsick . . ."

I turned as pale as a slice of provolone cheese. Turbulence? **BUMPY** ride? Airsick? Rotten ricotta, this didn't sound good! Plus, I'm afraid of heights! Before I had a chance to change my mind, the plane's engines were revving up, and we were racing down the runway and into the **SKY**!

The *plane* gained altitude, but it bounced

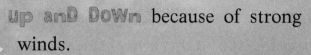 because of strong winds.

Next to me, Hercule calmly ate a banana. "Do you want one, Geronimo?" he asked me. "They're the perfect plane snack!"

Ugh. I couldn't eat a thing! "No thanks," I said weakly. "Maybe I'll just look out the window for a little while."

But as soon as I looked outside, the plane dipped suddenly. My stomach did flips and I started to sweat.

"**CHEER UP**, Geronimo," Hercule said, seeing the look on my snout. "I'm sure the ride will even out soon."

I grimaced. "I've **changed** my mind! I want to go home!" I cried.

"It's too late for that, SILLY mouse!" Hercule said. "Besides, it's just a storm. We'll be there in no time! To keep your mind off the flight, I will tell you stories from my **mouserific** family history. I once had an aunt who was so afraid to fly, that she swam everywhere she went!"

Thankfully, Hercule's story was so boring that I fell asleep. By the time I woke up, we were landing at Hilo's airport.

After we deplaned and picked up our luggage, Hercule searched the crowd for the mouse who was supposed to be meeting us. Fortunately, Hercule's distinctive, bright

yellow hat makes him easy to spot. We didn't wait **LONG**!

A tall, young mouselet, with long, dark fur, strode toward us. "You must be the famouse Hercule Poirat and Geronimo Stilton!" he cried. He squeezed each of our paws in hearty shakes.

"Jumping Jack cheese, you have a strong grip!" I groaned and cradled my paw.

"Aloha! My name is Makanakai, but everyone calls me Kai. My friend **KEALOHA** sent me to meet you. I'm going to be your guide while you're here!"

He grabbed a few of our bags and gestured to us to follow him. Strangely, he walked right past the parking lot and continued toward the beach.

Before I could ask what was happening,
Kai had ushered us onto Hilo's marina.

"Traveling to Kealoha's house will be much
faster by boat," he announced. In front of
us bobbed a blue speedboat, with Kai Travel
Tours and Tales! written on the side.

My whiskers quivered. I get seasick!

Kai loaded our luggage on his boat, not
noticing my anxiety. "I take tourists to all
of Hawaii's different islands and teach them

All aboard!

Thank you!

Ugh!

KAI TRAVEL
Tours and Tales!

things about Hawaii!" he explained.

Kai started the engine and we shot off into the sea. The boat rocked side to side through very tall waves, and I grabbed my stomach. I turned green from my ears to the tip of my tail!

Hercule happily reached into his bag for a snack. "Doesn't the sea air make you hungry, Geronimo?" he called to me. "Anyone want one of my bananas?"

I groaned, but Kai looked stern. "It's bad luck to eat bananas on a boat!" he told Hercule.

Hercule sighed. "I'm sorry. I'll wait until we go ashore to eat a snack."

"We'll be there soon!" Kai said. "But for now, just enjoy the natural beauty of HAWAII!"

The scenery was indeed mousetastic!

Rocky cliffs towered over white sand beaches, and the ocean glittered under bright **blue** skies. We sailed past the Kilauea VOLCANO. Glowing hot lava flowed down dark rocks all the way to the cold ocean, where it created a dramatic burst of STEAM.

"Wow! What a view!" Hercule and I exclaimed.

Wow!

What a view!

"I know many **folktales** about VOLCANOES," Kai said. "Would you like to hear one?"

"Volcanoes are nice, but my favorite thing in the world is bananas — do you know any stories about them?" Hercule asked.

Kai burst out laughing. "Sure! I do know a folktale about bananas."

KILAUEA VOLCANO

The Wonderful
BANANA PEEL

A long time ago there was a young mouse named Kukali who lived on one of the Hawaiian Islands. He was always very eager to travel. One day his father told him: "Kukali, it's time for you to fulfill your dreams." As a parting gift, his father gave him a special banana and told him not to throw away the peel after eating it.

Kukali said good-bye to his father and left. He walked all day through a thick forest. In the evening, he stopped to rest and ate the banana his father had given him. He saved the peel as his father had instructed and lay down to sleep. When he woke up the following day, the peel was not empty anymore. Inside was a whole new banana!

Kukali built a canoe and sailed far away across the ocean. Finally, he came to an island and rowed his canoe ashore. Tired from his journey, he fell into a deep sleep.

He slept so soundly that he did not wake up when the giant bird who ruled this island swooped down and carried him to a valley. When Kukali awoke, he found himself surrounded by a group of very hungry mice.

They explained that the bird had mousenapped them and was keeping them prisoner in the valley without any food. They feared the bird was planning to eat them! Kukali decided to share the magical banana his father had given him. All of the mice were able to eat because the peel kept refilling with fresh fruit!

Once they had their strength back, the prisoners of the island were able to defeat the giant bird and return home. They were forever thankful for Kukali — and his magical banana peel!

HAWAIIAN
WORDS AND PHRASES

ĀKAMAI: smart

ALOHA: hello, good-bye, love, affection

HALE: house

HAUʻOLI LĀ HĀNĀ: Happy birthday

HOALOHA: friend

HONU: turtle

Iʻa: fish

KAI: sea

KUMU: teacher

KUPUNA: grandparent or ancestor

LIMU: seaweed

LUAU: Hawaiian feast

MAHALO: thanks

MAIKAʻI NO MAHALO: Fine indeed, thank you

MANŌ: shark

MOANA: ocean

NIU: coconut

PEHEA ʻOE: How are you?

KEALOHA ON
THE CLIFFS

As we left the open sea and approached a small dock, Kai pointed out a **HOUSE ON a CLIFF.**

"That's Kealoha's house. Her jewelry **studio** is there, but her store is in Honolulu, on Oahu."

After we docked the boat, we walked to the house and Kai rang the bell. When no one answered, he called out: "**KEALOHA!**"

There was no reply, but Kai only shrugged. "She might be walking around looking for inspiration. Let's go find her, I know all her favorite places."

"Have you known each other for a long time?" I asked Kai.

"We have been friends since we were baby

mouselets!" he said.

Hercule and I followed Kai around the corner, past a small village main street and toward a 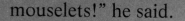beautiful white sand beach. There by the water stood a young rodent holding a sketchbook. She was wearing a blue dress embroidered with starfish, and a white orchid in her long, black fur.

"Kealoha, over here!" Kai called, blushing all the way to the tips of his whiskers.

She walked toward us and smiled, extending her paw. "I'm so glad you're here!

I hope you can help me." She shook her head sadly. "Let's go up to the house, and I'll tell you more about the necklace."

"What were you drawing?" I asked, curious, as we headed back the way we came.

She opened her sketchbook as we walked. "I'm working on a design for a pair of earrings. I'm finding it hard to concentrate in the HOUSE because of all the attempted break-ins!" Her whiskers drooped.

Kai looked concerned. "I don't want to add to your troubles," he said. "But I thought you'd want to see this." He pulled a NEWSPAPER article from his back pocket.

Kealoha frowned as she read the article. "I'm so happy and grateful to be making the wedding jewelry, but I don't like this kind of publicity! I wanted mouselets to hear about my work in a positive way. And I

GOSSIP! GOSSIP!

STARS TO WED ON THE BIG ISLAND!

By Chet Cheddar

The much-anticipated wedding of the famouse actors Violet Brie and Roderick van Ratten will finally take place tomorrow on the Big Island.

But there's drama brewing! Van Ratten wanted to commission a special piece of jewelry to give Brie on their big day. Rumor has it that his first stop was the famous Madame No of EGO Corp.

But just as they were about to shake paws on a deal, Van Ratten came across the work of up-and-coming young rodent Kealoha. He couldn't decide between the two talents — so he hired both of them!

But only one necklace can be the official gift — and it turns out Kealoha's was the winner!

Word on the street is that Madame No is seeing red. She's not used to being beat out by lesser-known designers. Has the wedding of the century created the feud of the century? We'll find out!

had no **idea** that Madame No would take losing our friendly competition so badly!" She handed the paper back to Kai.

KEALOHA led us through the village and into her house. She offered us glasses of sweet pineapple juice and bowls of haupia, a delicious coconut pudding.

While we were enjoying our snack, she took out photos of the fabumouse necklace she'd crafted for the wedding.

"We are keeping it in the Honolulu store for safekeeping," she said.

Holey Swiss cheese, the necklace was

mousetacular! It was made to look like a Hawaiian lei, and the jeweled flowers in the garland were so sparkly they almost glowed. The

delicate clasp at the top of the necklace had an inscription that read, *Our love is as beautiful as a flower.*

As we were marveling over the necklace, Kai brought out some more photos.

"Here are the images from the store cameras," he said. "Someone broke in three times but was never able to open the locked display case where the necklace is kept."

"Thankfully they couldn't figure out the code," Kealoha said.

First they tried the window . . .

Then they tried the gate . . .

Finally, they tried to deactivate the alarm . . .

"It's 'ALOHA,'" Kai blurted out. He blushed red from his tail to the tips of his ears. "Oops, I shouldn't have said that." He looked over at Kealoha, but she only smiled.

"It's okay. They should know the code anyway," she said.

Hercule poured over the surveillance photos with his magnifying glass. "The thief was clever enough to avoid having his snout captured by the cameras. But look! In this photo, you can see a little bit of sleeve . . . the rodent is wearing a pink wet suit!"

"The Super Surfer race will be taking place soon on Oahu Island," Kealoha said. "The starting line is right by my store."

I stroked my whiskers. "Could the thief be posing as one of the competitors?" I wondered aloud.

"I have an idea!" Hercule squeaked. "Geronimo will sign up for this **Super Surfer** race so that he can blend in with the other competitors and keep an eye on your store."

"Moldy mozzarella, I'm a **mouse**, not a fish!" I cried. "I don't know how to surf!"

"Don't worry," Kai said. He patted me on the back. "I will **TEACH** you everything you need to know!"

He looked confident, but I was *shaking* in my **fur**.

Hercule stood and gestured to me. "Come on, Geronimo, time to go! I need a nap — and maybe a nice piece of cheesy toast to get my brain working."

I sighed, waved GOOD-BYE to Kai and Kealoha, and followed Hercule out of the house. What had I gotten myself into?!

You Call This a Vacation?!

The next morning, I woke up and stretched my **paws** over my head. The smell of the ocean coming in my window was so refreshing, I almost forgot I had a case to help solve.

I started *flipping through* the tourist brochure that was sitting on my nightstand.

That looks fun!

Might as well try and relax, now that I was here!

"This first thing I'll do is breakfast, then I'll go to the spa, and after that I'll take a walk on the beach," I decided. "Maybe I'll try some delicious local food for lunch. I've heard the pineapple cheese is out of this world!"

Breakfast in bed!

A relaxing massage!

I had just picked up the phone to call **room service** when I heard a knock on my door and Hercule's voice boomed into my room. "Are you

Yum!

still in bed, you **LAZY** mouse! Kai is here to give you a **Surfing lesson!**"

Rancid rat tails! I opened the door and Hercule grabbed my paw. "Hurry up!" he cried, pulling me down the hall. Behind me, I heard the door *slam* shut. I was locked out! And I was still wearing my PAJAMAS!

"Wait!" I cried.

But Hercule was not **listening**. He dragged me all the way to the beach, where **KAI** was waiting for us.

Just then a group of tourists from Mouse Island walked by us, giggling.

"Isn't that the famouse reporter, *Geronimo Stilton*?" I heard a mouse whisper. "What a funny-looking swimsuit!"

I groaned and covered my snout with my paws, but Kai laughed. "Don't worry, Geronimo. I have extra swim trunks you can borrow." He dug around in his knapsack and pulled out an ENORMOUSE pair of

shorts. "Hurry and put these on so we can start our lesson!"

If only he knew I was in no hurry! But I accepted the swim trunks and went to change.

When I returned, Kai had set two SURFBOARDS in the sand. Hercule lounged nearby on a towel, eating the snacks he had brought with him.

"Nice outfit," Hercule called and I **scowled**.

"Don't pay any attention to him," Kai said. "Come try out your board!"

I trudged through the sand and placed a tentative paw onto my surfboard. Slimy Swiss cheese, how do I let Hercule talk me into things like this?

But Kai was a good teacher. He had me

Like this.

Oops!

lie down on the board and practice getting up into a standing position. Over and over and OVER again. He really worked my whiskers off! Soon, I was **sweatier** than a cheese slice left out in the sun. But Kai was only just getting started.

"Now let's try out your new moves on some real **waves**!" he said. "Just remember to stay away from the coral. It's very sharp and can slice your tail off! And when we get close to the reef, keep an eye out for moray eels. They can bite you. Oh, and most of all, watch out for the JELLYFISH. If they sting you, it will burn like crazy!"

"Thundering cattails, is that all — or is there anything else that can kill me?"

JELLYFISH

"Of course not!" Kai ruffled the **fur** on my head. "Except for **SHARKS**. But don't be a **worryrat**. You'll see their fins coming from a mile away!"

SQUEAK!

"I've changed my mind. Surfing's not for me. I don't want to be **sliced**, **zapped**, **stung**, or **eaten up**! I just want to sunbathe on the beach!"

SHARKS

Kai burst out laughing. "It's too late to get **cold paws**, Geronimo! You'll be fine, I promise!"

"I believe in you, Geronimo!" Hercule called from his beach towel. He flipped through the mystery novel he had brought with him and took a bite of **banana**.

I was outnumbered! Reluctantly, I waded into the **WATER** and for the next

FLOATER
Riding the wave as it's about to break

TUBE RIDING
Riding inside the "tube" created by a wave

few hours, ran drills with Kai. I waited for **waves** and tried to stand up on my board.

It didn't go well. I couldn't catch any waves!

Finally, a **perfect wave** approached and Kai and I paddled out. "This is it! You can do it!" he called to me. I timed it out and jumped to standing, just as Kai had taught me.

"I'm doing it!" I yelled. But my HAPPINESS quickly turned to TERROR as I felt a sharp stinging sensation on my tail.

Help!

Ha, ha, ha!

"HELP! A jellyfish stung me! Call 911!" I squeaked.

"It's just me, Geronimo!" Hercule floated by my surfboard wearing a jellyfish hat. "See?" He held up a stick he had used to POKE my tail.

"Not funny!" I huffed, and I swam back to shore. As I approached our spot on the sand, I noticed Kealoha had arrived to check out our progress. She was sitting on the beach sketching. As I got close, I could see she'd sketched Kai riding a big wave.

"Hello, Kealoha," I called, and she closed her sketchbook abruptly, blushing.

"Why hello, Geronimo! Are you a Super Surfer yet?"

I shrugged. "Keep your paws crossed for me tomorrow!"

I'd need all the luck I could get!

DON'T BE SUCH A SCAREDY-MOUSE!

The following day Kai drove us to the airport. We were going to fly to Oahu, where the Super Surfer race was taking place.

We drove past two active volcanoes, Mauna Loa and Kilauea.

"I don't think I have ever been this close to a real VOLCANO before!" I said.

"I know many legends about volcanoes —
I'll tell you one later on our trip!"

When we got to the airport, Kai parked
his jeep and walked us over to a small blue
PLANE with the name Kai Travel Tours
and Tales! painted on its side.

My whiskers trembled. "Is that thing
strong enough to carry all of us?" I asked.

"Of course!" Kai said. "I'm going to fly

PELE AND VOLCANOS

Pele, the fire Goddess, had a fight with her sister Namakaokaha'i. Because of this, her father sent her off, with only a canoe, in search of a new home.

Pele visited many islands and territories. In each, she dug a firepit for a new home, but every time, her sister found her and extinguished the flames. Pele made her way through the chain of Hawaiian islands, creating the Haleakala volcano on Maui. Here her sister found her and they had a fight to the death. Pele's mortal form died, but she became a goddess and traveled to the Big Island. Here she dug her final firepit, the Halemaumau Crater at the summit of Kilauea, where she stayed.

you myself. I do it all the time!"

Hercule and I climbed aboard. I fastened my seat belt extra tight as Kai started the engine. "If we run into **TROUBLE**, you can always bail out in the ocean!" Kai bellowed over the noise.

Rat-munching rattlesnakes!

The flight was **BUMPY**, but short. At the airport, there were lots of athletic-looking mice wearing **Super Surfer** gear.

We followed the group outside to a bus headed to the race site and climbed aboard.

Once we got to the *beach*, I nervously approached the race sign-up table. As I waited my turn, one of the race organizers handed me a program.

Yikes! This was not going to be easy! Words jumped out at me: **DANGEROUS! SHARKS! FOR SUPER MICE ONLY!**

My whiskers *shook* with fear. That was it — I was out!

But just then someone **tapped** me on my shoulder.

"*Geronimo Stilton!* Are you also joining the Super Surfer race?"

I turned around to see a tall mouselet wearing a **pink** wet suit.

"We met at a party for your newspaper back on Mouse Island," she explained. "But

maybe you don't remember?" Her whiskers DROOPED.

"Of course I remember you!" I cried, wracking my CHEDDARBRAIN. She did seem familiar, but I couldn't quite place her. She extended her paw. "It's all right. My name is Grace Cheesington. I'm a

Super Surfer
Race Registration

Geronimo
Stilton!

HUGE fan of *The Rodent's Gazette*. Such marvemouse reporting!"

I blushed from the tip of my tail to the tops of my ears.

"And now it turns out you're also a **super** mouse!" She gestured to the sign-up sheet.

I gulped. I couldn't walk AWAY now!

Not with my **biggest** fan watching! I hastily **scrawled** my name on the sheet and gave the pen to Grace.

"How long have you been **training** for this?" Grace asked as she signed her name and took a **program** from the organizers.

"Well, uh, not too long . . ." I **trailed** off. I didn't want to lie, but I didn't want her to know I was a rookie! As I was struggling to find the right words, ① I tripped over my own tail — and ② fell right into a case of FRESHLY CAUGHT FISH!

Oops!

What a smell!

I tried to get up, but I slipped and **SLAMMED** my snout into a greased

SURFBOARD. ③ I twirled up in the air and I did a TRIPLE BACK-FLIP with a double twist. By sheer luck, I landed on my knees right in front of her! "Just limbering up for the big race!" I said and chuckled.

Oh no!

OFF TO HONOLULU!

I was so embarrassed, but I tried not to show it. I casually pulled an **anchovy** out of my ear. "I never did like **seafood**!"

Grace giggled. "You are really **funny**, Mr. Stilton!"

"No need to be so formal, you can call me Stilton — I mean Mister — I mean *Geronimo*!"

Grace batted her EYELASHES. "Geronimo it is, then! Tell me, Geronimo, is this your first time in **HAWAII**?"

"**YES**, it is. A friend thought I needed a vacation." I had to be careful that I didn't mention the **REAL** reason I was here!

"Have you been to Honolulu yet?" Grace asked. "I want to **squeeze** in a quick visit before the race starts this afternoon. I hear there's a MARVEMOUSE fondue restaurant — and a *wonderful* little jewelry boutique. Perhaps you could come with me! We could do some **sightseeing** right now!"

I wiped a stray anchovy off my glasses. I really wanted to go, but the race started soon . . . "Well, if it's a quick trip," I said. I might as well have a little **fun** while I was in **HAWAII**!

Grace **wrapped** a cover-up around her wet suit and we headed away from the **BEACH**.

As Grace and I

Let's go to Honolulu!

Umm . . .

stepped off the beach, we ran into Hercule and Kai.

"Where are you going?" Hercule cried. The **RACE** starts in three hours! Don't you want to do some LAST-MINUTE practicing with Kai?"

I squinted my eyes and gestured for Hercule to stop talking. I didn't want Grace to know I didn't know how to **SURF**! She admired me! "Don't be such a cheesebrain, Hercule! I'm just taking a trip into Honolulu. I'll be back, quick as a whisker!"

Grace took me on a **whirlwind** tour of all of Honolulu's famouse sites. We walked by **Iolani Palace**. We admired the **STATUE** of **KING KAMEHAMEHA** and the **ALOHA TOWER**.

Finally, we took a walk in the shopping district past lots of beautiful stores.

THE CITY OF HONOLULU

THE STATUE OF KING KAMEHAMEHA

King Kamehameha was the first king to rule over all the Hawaiian Islands. This statue is one of Hawaii's most famouse landmarks.

THE IOLANI PALACE

This palace, completed in 1882 during King Kalakaua's rule, is one of only two existing royal residences in the United States.

THE ALOHA TOWER

The Aloha Tower is Honolulu's lighthouse. It's been guiding vessels into the city's port since 1926.

Grace stopped in front of a sign that read: **Kealoha Jewelry**.

It was Kealoha's store!

"Oh, here is the boutique I heard about!" Grace **SQUEAKED**. "Let's go in and take a quick **PEEK**!"

"Kealoha is a good friend of mine!" I bragged. "She designed a beautiful necklace for Roderick van Ratten and Violet Brie's WEDDING."

Grace clasped her paws in front of her. "Ohhhh, really? Would you introduce me? I would **really** love to meet her and see the necklace!"

"Let's see if she's in!" I held open the door for Grace and followed her into the store.

Kealoha hadn't arrived yet, but while we **WAITED**, one of the shop mice led me over to the locked display case.

"The system is state-of-the-art," I informed her. "Only a few rodents have the code . . . including me!" I couldn't help but tell her.

"Wow," Grace whispered. "How impressive that she trusts you with something so **VALUABLE**."

I blushed.

"Such a one-of-a-kind piece," Grace said, peering through the glass. "Do you think I could try it on — just for a MOMENT?"

My stomach **flip-flopped**. "Oh, um, I don't think so . . ." I said.

"Please, Geronimo?" she asked. "I think it will give me good luck for the big race!"

THE RACE! I had forgotten all about it. Maybe I should try on the necklace, too, if it would give me good luck!

I AM A CHEDDARBRAIN!

I caved like a cheese soufflé. "Okay, I guess a *quick* look can't hurt."

Grace grinned. "I'll be careful, I promise!" She hovered close to me as I racked my brain to remember the password. Sliced Swiss cheese, what was it?

Oh, right! I activated the keypad, moved to block Grace's view, and typed it in: ALOHA

The display buzzed loudly, and for a moment I was worried I had entered the password incorrectly. Were security mice about to swoop in and arrest me? My whiskers twitched at the thought.

But slowly the buzzing subsided and

I heard a **CLANK**! The display case door swung open.

Carefully, I picked up the sparkling necklace and fastened it around Grace's neck. It was even more *incredimouse* than it had looked through the glass.

I stepped back to admire the way the

Here you go!

jeweled flowers **glittered** in the shop lights.

But as soon as I did, Grace's smile turned **upside down**.

"Thanks for your help, Stilton!" she sneered.

Thanks, Stilt

To my astonishment, she reached up and pulled off her **red** wig, revealing long blond locks underneath. Then she popped out a set of contacts to reveal **ICY BLUE** eyes. Finally, she peeled off a mask — Grace Cheesington's entire appearance had been an elaborate **LIE**!

"**Jumping Jack cheese, you're Shadow!**" I squeaked. Shadow and I had crossed paths before. She was Madame

No's SUPERSPY!

"So nice to see you again, Geronimo," she said, slipping the necklace into her pocket. "Sorry I can't stay to chat!"

Before I could move a WHiSKeR, she had raced out of the shop and DISAPPEARED into the crowd outside.

Just then Kealoha came into the shop. "Oh good, just the mouse I wanted to see," she said, spotting me.

"No time to talk!" I **squeaked**, my senses returning. "I have to follow Shadow! She's taken the necklace!" I rushed past her and ran in the direction I had seen Shadow DISAPPEAR. This was all my fault — I had to catch her!

What happened?

SQUEAK, A SHARK!

I *raced* through the shopping district, occasionally catching glimpses of Shadow's pink wet suit. It seemed like she was heading back to the start of the **Super Surfer** race. She'd be hard to spot in a crowd of mice also wearing wet suits.

Wait! Stop!

SUPER S

I huffed and puffed my way down to the beach just in time to see Shadow throw off her cover-up and jump into the water with a surfboard.

A voice **boomed** from above: "Super Surfers, it's time for the main event! Get swimming to Shark Rocks to pick up your boards!"

The crowd of surfers **cheered** and started running to the beach. In all the chaos, I was swept up with them!

"Wait! Stop!" I cried, but they didn't seem to **HEAR** me.

The Super Surfers dragged me all the way into the **ocean**. One by one, they jogged into the water and started SWIMMING. Meanwhile, Shadow was already so far ahead she looked like a small dot on the *horizon*.

"Greasy cat guts!" I **sighed**, waves lapping at my knees. "I'll never catch up! The necklace is **LOST**!"

Just as I was about to head back to dry land, I caught the shape of a fin out of the corner of my eye.

SQUEAK! A SHARK!

Shaaaaaaaaaaark!

I took off like a rocket and plunged back into the *waves*. I've never swam so fast in all my life! When I reached **SHARK ROCKS**, I finally stopped to catch my breath.

But someone else had also stopped to catch her breath . . . Shadow!

"Stop right there, fontina face!" I shouted.

But she jumped in the water with her surfboard and started surfing toward **Wind Rocks**! I had no choice but to follow her.

I spotted my surfboard on one of the rocks with the ones belonging to all the other racers. It was now or never — had Kai taught me enough about surfing?

Thankfully, it seemed to go okay! I managed to catch a wave and ride it all the way to Wind Rocks!

Shadow finally came into view. Her wave had died out, and she was paddling furiously.

"STOP, THIEF!" I shouted. My wave died out, too, and I was forced to start paddling as well. But suddenly, the SEA shifted and a gigantic wave rose up over both of us. "Hold on!" I cried, grabbing Shadow's paw. "It's the only way we'll make it!" She held on tightly, but just as we went underwater, I spotted Kealoha's one-of-a-kind necklace fall out of her POCKET.

SQUEAK! No!

YOU AGAIN, STILTON?

Shadow pawed around under the water for a while, trying to reach the necklace. I held on to her paw so she wouldn't drift away with the current. When we finally surfaced, I pulled SHADOW on my surfboard to the safety of SHALLOW water.

Gasp!

"This isn't over, Stilton," she said.

Shadow pulled a waterproof remote control from her wet suit pocket and pressed a button. The ocean started to froth and swirl, and a leopard-print submarine popped up out of the water. A hatch opened and the rotten rodent, MADAME NO herself, appeared.

"Did you get the necklace?" she called.

Did you get the necklace?

Madame No's SUBMARINE

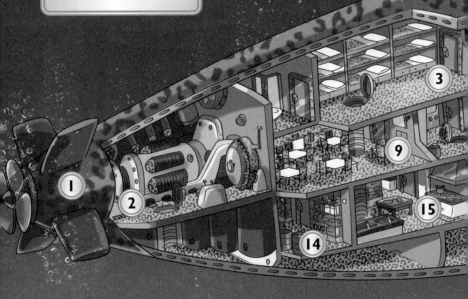

Madame No!

Madame No is the Mega Director of the EGO: the Enormously Gigantic Organization. This powerful company delves into many kinds of businesses, both honest and shady. Ask her a question, and she only has one answer: NO!

Shadow shook her head. "I had it in my paws, but Stilton, the cheddarhead, made me drop it into the ocean!"

"Not you again, Stilton!" Madame No SHOUTED angrily. But then a STRANGE smile came over her face. "At least Kealoha won't be able to deliver it to the wedding of the century. Her reputation will be RUINED!" Madame No cackled.

"Cat got your tongue?" Shadow hissed at me as I stared dumbfounded at Madame No. "Oh, well, until we meet again!" she said and swam toward the submarine. She clambered up the side, and she and Madame No DISAPPEARED inside.

With a whir, the submarine descended back under the WATER.

The submarine's descent created a gigantic wave and I went tail over ears through the **WATER** — all the way back to the **Super Surfer** race's starting area. I had completed the whole race! But I didn't feel like celebrating. Kealoha's necklace was lost FOREVER, and there was nothing I could do about it!

Sob!
Sob!

WE WANT YOU ANYWAY!

Hercule, Kealoha, and Kai RAN toward me across the BEACH. By the look on their faces, I knew that Kealoha's staff must have filled them in on Shadow's deception.

"Geronimo! Did you get the necklace back from Shadow?" Hercule asked.

I couldn't help but let out a sob. "I am so sorry! She tricked me! I caught up to her, but the necklace . . . it — it — it — it fell into the ocean!" I covered my snout with my paws.

I thought Kealoha would be mad. I had unlocked her safe for a world-famouse thief in disguise! But she just hugged me. "Don't CRY, Geronimo," she said.

"There's something you should know. The necklace in the store display wasn't the real one. **IT WAS A FAKE!**"

My mouth dropped open. "**A FAKE?**" I cried.

"Yes! That's the one I made to show Roderick what the finished necklace would look like. With all the ROBBERY attempts, I thought it would be a good idea to **SECRETLY** swap the real one for a decoy in the store," Kealoha explained. "The real necklace is back at my house."

"That's **tremendmouse!**" Kai cried. "You're **brilliant!**"

Kealoha blushed. But then she grew serious. "The **wedding** starts in two hours. We'll have to hurry if we want to deliver the real necklace on time!"

"*Let's go, then!*" Hercule cried.

Together we took off running across the beach as fast as our **paws** could carry us. We had to get to the **airport** so Kai could fly us back to Hilo. I didn't relish the thought of going up in a plane again, but I'd do anything to help save Kealoha's career!

We flew to **Hilo**, and then Kai drove us to Kealoha's house in his jeep.

Puff!
Puff!

Hurry!

Follow me!

Kealoha ran to her room and pulled the necklace out of a hidden compartment in one of her dresser drawers. "I just had a **feeling** it would be safest here," she said **TRIUMPHANTLY**. "If I'd left it in the store display, it would be gone **forever**!"

My whiskers trembled. It would have been all my fault! But there was no time to be a worryrat now. We had a **wedding** to get to!

"Back to the plane, RODENTS!" Hercule squeaked. "There's no time to lose!"

We ran out of the house, piled into Kai's jeep, and raced all the way back to the airport. As the plane took off, rain started to pelt the runway.

Rancid rat hairs! We were in for a bumpy ride . . .

The rain poured down, and the wind

blew us from *side to side*. My stomach churned. Kai managed to set the plane back down at the Honolulu airport and we climbed out.

"Let's go!" Kai cried. "The CEREMONY is about to start, but I think we can just make it!"

He and Kealoha took off **running** while I stopped for a moment to catch my BREATH. Hadn't I *RACED* enough today?!

Hercule grabbed my 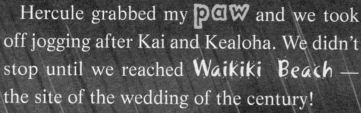 and we took off jogging after Kai and Kealoha. We didn't stop until we reached **Waikiki Beach** — the site of the wedding of the century!

There, a who's who of rodents sheltered under a tent, waiting for the storm to blow

CEREMONY

over. The wedding hadn't started yet! We had done it!

Kealoha ducked under the tent and presented the necklace to Roderick. "I'm so sorry I'm late . . . the RAIN delayed us!"

"Don't worry, Kealoha! The rain delayed us, too!" he said with a laugh.

Hercule, Kai, and I stepped under the tent just as Roderick lifted the necklace up to Violet. "This is for you," he said. "I'm the happiest mouse in the world today because we're getting married." He fastened the glittering jewels around her neck.

"It's fabumouse!" Violet squeaked.

I had to agree. Even though the decoy necklace had seemed INCREDIMOUSE back at the store, I could see now it had been a pale slice of cheese compared to the real thing. Kealoha was a true artist.

Mouserific News

Thankfully, the rain ended quickly and the SUN came out. Violet Brie and Roderick van Ratten invited us to stay for the **wedding**, and we *happily* accepted. It's not every day you get invited to the wedding of the century!

After the ceremony, there was MUSIC, traditional Hawaiian dancers, and lots of delicious food.

I wandered down to the BEACH and spotted Kealoha sitting with her sketchpad. She had a small smile on her face as she sketched some happy partygoers. Everymouse was having fun, but I felt a little bit SAD.

I couldn't believe I had fallen for Shadow's

SILLY disguise. What a cheddarhead! I had almost ruined the wedding. I sighed.

"You look like someone just ate the last wheel of Brie!" Kai said, coming up behind me. "Why so GLOOMY, Geronimo?" he asked, putting a paw on my shoulder.

"I'm okay. I just can't believe I almost RUINED things for Kealoha."

"But you didn't!" Kai said. "To take your mind off things, try some of this RICE SALAD and lobster tail — I brought it over just for you!" Kai offered me the bowl.

Why so gloomy?

I noticed Kai was STARING at Kealoha, and I handed it back to him. "Why

Hawaiian Specialties

Ask an adult to help you!

RICE SALAD IN GRAPEFRUIT CUPS

INGREDIENTS:

2 pink grapefruits, 1 cup rice, stuffed olives, 1 pickled red pepper, 1 lemon, olive oil, 1 tsp curry powder

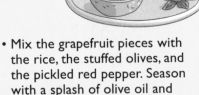

- With the help of an adult, cut the grapefruits in half and scoop the fruit out of the rind. Make sure the rind stays intact. Cut the grapefruit and red pepper into small pieces.

- Ask an adult to cook the rice according to the directions on the package.

- Mix the grapefruit pieces with the rice, the stuffed olives, and the pickled red pepper. Season with a splash of olive oil and lemon juice and a teaspoon of curry powder. Mix well and stuff it into the grapefruit rinds.

SERVES FOUR

MELON AND LOBSTER SALAD

INGREDIENTS:

1 hard, ripe melon, lobster tails, fresh cream, minced parsley

Ask an adult to help cut the melon in half. Scoop out the seeds, carefully take out the flesh, and cut into pieces. Do not discard the rind. Pour the cream in a bowl, and add the minced parsley. Ask an adult to boil the lobster tails in lightly salted water. Drain them and refrigerate until cold. When the tails have chilled completely, shell them and chop the lobster meat. In a large salad bowl, gently toss the lobster with the cream and minced parsley and add the melon. Place salad into the saved melon rinds and refrigerate for 30 minutes before serving.

SERVES FOUR

don't you go see if Kealoha wants some, instead," I suggested, nudging him with my ELBOW.

Kai blushed, his fur turning PiNK all the way to his toes: "I don't know what to say! I don't think I can do it."

I straightened up. "Kai, I barely know how to surf and I completed a Super Surfer race today. You can talk to Kealoha, even if you're not sure what to say. Why don't you start by asking her about her drawing?"

Kai took a deep breath. "I can do that," he said seriously, and I chuckled. Kai went to talk to Kealoha and I headed back to the BUFFET to try some of that rice salad he had offered me. I ran right into an EXCITED-looking Hercule.

"Holey Swiss cheese! I just heard mouserific news!" He grabbed my paw and JUMPED up and down.

"Hercule, calm down! What on EARTH are you talking about?" But before he could answer, a voice boomed behind me.

"Are you Geronimo Stilton?"

It was one of the Super Surfer race organizers, soaked from the tips of his ears to the tip of his tail, holding a huge, shiny trophy.

As soon as I nodded, he breathed a sigh of relief. "I have been chasing you down all day! I was even caught in the rain! Do you want this TROPHY or not?"

"What trophy?" I asked.

"The Super Surfer trophy, of course! You WON the race! You got to the finish line ten minutes before everyone else. You were going so fast we thought you were being chased by a shark!"

I laughed nervously and held my **paws** out for the trophy. I couldn't believe I had actually **WON**!

The organizer **clapped** his paws to get everyone's attention. "Mouselets, please join me in congratulating our **Super Surfer** — Geronimo Stilton!"

To my embarrassment, everyone had gathered around to see what was going on. "Um, thanks," I said. "I couldn't have done it without my old friend Hercule, who urged me to go on a **HAWAIIAN** vacation. And I definitely couldn't have done it without my new friend Kai — the best surf instructor in all of **HAWAII**!"

Everyone **cheered**. "Congratulations to the **happy** couple," I continued. "May your years together be as **fabumouse** as Kealoha's wedding necklace."

Everyone cheered again, and the party resumed.

I guess I *had* needed a vacation. And what a **VACATION** it had been! Now that the necklace was safe and sound, maybe I could finally **ReLaX** a little and enjoy the beautiful landscape.

I wandered down to the beach and saw that Kai and Kealoha had beat me to it. But I didn't mind. I was **happy** to see my two new favorite mice had found each other.

ALOHA!

Don't miss a single fabumouse adventure!

Up Next:

Don't miss any of these exciting Thea Sisters adventures!

Thea Stilton and the Dragon's Code

Thea Stilton and the Mountain of Fire

Thea Stilton and the Ghost of the Shipwreck

Thea Stilton and the Secret City

Thea Stilton and the Mystery in Paris

Thea Stilton and the Cherry Blossom Adventure

Thea Stilton and the Star Castaways

Thea Stilton: Big Trouble in the Big Apple

Thea Stilton and the Ice Treasure

Thea Stilton and the Secret of the Old Castle

Thea Stilton and the Blue Scarab Hunt

Thea Stilton and the Prince's Emerald

Thea Stilton and the Mystery on the Orient Express

Thea Stilton and the Dancing Shadows

Thea Stilton and the Legend of the Fire Flowers

Thea Stilton and the Spanish Dance Mission

Thea Stilton and the Journey to the Lion's Den

Thea Stilton and the Great Tulip Heist

Thea Stilton and the Chocolate Sabotage

Thea Stilton and the Missing Myth

Thea Stilton and the Lost Letters

Thea Stilton and the Tropical Treasure

Thea Stilton and the Hollywood Hoax

Thea Stilton and the Madagascar Madness

Thea Stilton and the Frozen Fiasco

Thea Stilton and the Venice Masquerade

Thea Stilton and the Niagara Splash

Thea Stilton and the Riddle of the Ruins

Thea Stilton and the Phantom of the Orchestra

Thea Stilton and the Black Forest Burglary

And check out my fabumouse special editions!

THEA STILTON: THE JOURNEY TO ATLANTIS

THEA STILTON: THE SECRET OF THE FAIRIES

THEA STILTON: THE SECRET OF THE SNOW

THEA STILTON: THE CLOUD CASTLE

THEA STILTON: THE TREASURE OF THE SEA

THEA STILTON: THE LAND OF FLOWERS

THEA STILTON: THE SECRET OF THE CRYSTAL FAIRIES

About the Author

Born in New Mouse City, Mouse Island, **GERONIMO STILTON** is Rattus Emeritus of Mousomorphic Literature and of Neo-Ratonic Comparative Philosophy. For the past twenty years, he has been running *The Rodent's Gazette,* New Mouse City's most widely read daily newspaper.

Stilton was awarded the Ratitzer Prize for his scoops on *The Curse of the Cheese Pyramid* and *The Search for Sunken Treasure.* He has also received the Andersen 2000 Prize for Personality of the Year. One of his bestsellers won the 2002 eBook Award for world's best ratlings' electronic book. His works have been published all over the globe.

In his spare time, Mr. Stilton collects antique cheese rinds and plays golf. But what he most enjoys is telling stories to his nephew Benjamin.

1. Main entrance
2. Printing presses (where the books and newspaper are printed)
3. Accounts department
4. Editorial room (where the editors, illustrators, and designers work)
5. Geronimo Stilton's office
6. Helicopter landing pad

THE RODENT'S GAZETTE

Map of New Mouse City

Map of Mouse Island

1. Big Ice Lake
2. Frozen Fur Peak
3. Slipperyslopes Glacier
4. Coldcreeps Peak
5. Ratzikistan
6. Transratania
7. Mount Vamp
8. Roastedrat Volcano
9. Brimstone Lake
10. Poopedcat Pass
11. Stinko Peak
12. Dark Forest
13. Vain Vampires Valley
14. Goose Bumps Gorge
15. The Shadow Line Pass
16. Penny Pincher Castle
17. Nature Reserve Park
18. Las Ratayas Marinas
19. Fossil Forest
20. Lake Lake
21. Lake Lakelake
22. Lake Lakelakelake
23. Cheddar Crag
24. Cannycat Castle
25. Valley of the Giant Sequoia
26. Cheddar Springs
27. Sulfurous Swamp
28. Old Reliable Geyser
29. Vole Vale
30. Ravingrat Ravine
31. Gnat Marshes
32. Munster Highlands
33. Mousehara Desert
34. Oasis of the Sweaty Camel
35. Cabbagehead Hill
36. Rattytrap Jungle
37. Rio Mosquito

Dear mouse friends,
Thanks for reading, and farewell
till the next book.
It'll be another whisker-licking-good
adventure, and that's a promise!

Geronimo Stilton